Magic Hearts

Candy Fairies

Magic Hearts

HELEN PERELMAN

ILLUSTRATED BY
ERICA-JANE WATERS

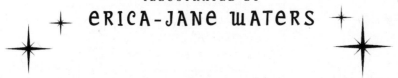

ALADDIN
NEW YORK   LONDON   TORONTO   SYDNEY   NEW DELHI

ALADDIN

An imprint of Simon & Schuster Children's Publishing Division

1230 Avenue of the Americas, New York, NY 10020

First Aladdin hardcover edition July 2013

Text copyright © 2011 by Helen Perelman

Illustrations copyright © 2011 by Erica-Jane Waters

Also available in Aladdin paperback edition.

For information about special discounts for bulk purchases, please contact
Simon & Schuster Special Sales at 1-866-506-1949 or business@simonandschuster.com.

The Simon & Schuster Speakers Bureau can bring authors to your live event.
For more information or to book an event contact the Simon & Schuster Speakers Bureau
at 1-866-248-3049 or visit our website at www.simonspeakers.com.

Designed by Karin Paprocki

The text of this book was set in Berthold Baskerville Book.

Manufactured in the United States of America 0613 FFG

2 4 6 8 10 9 7 5 3 1

Library of Congress Control Number 2010002494

ISBN 978-1-4424-6494-0 (hc)

ISBN 978-1-4424-0823-4 (pbk)

ISBN 978-1-4424-0824-1 (eBook)

For Danielle, my sweet niece!

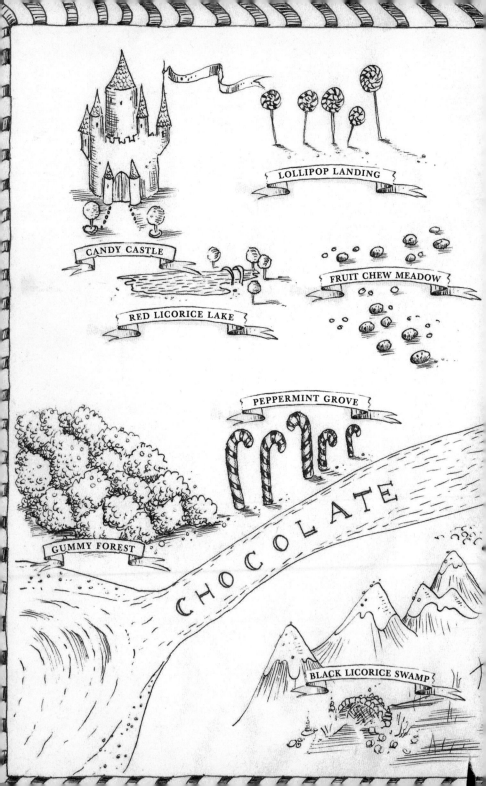

Contents

Magic Hearts

CHAPTER 1

A New Fairy Friend

What do you think?" Berry held up a string of colorful fruit chews. The Fruit Fairy enjoyed making <u>delicious</u> fruit candies, but she also loved making jewelry. The more sparkle the better! Berry loved anything and everything to do with fashion.

"Berry," Raina said. She had a worried look

on her face. The Gummy Fairy was filling up a bottle of cherry syrup for the trees in Gummy Forest. She had come to Fruit Chew Meadow for flavoring for the red gumdrop trees—and to visit Berry. But instead of finding Berry working on her fruit candies, her friend was making a necklace!

"Those are round chews," Raina said. "Where are the hearts?"

Berry shrugged. "These round fruit chews are just so pretty," she said with a heavy sigh. She held up the colorful strand again and admired the rainbow pattern she had made. "I just had to make a necklace with them!" She carefully knotted the end of the string. Then she put on a special caramel clasp that Melli, her Caramel Fairy friend, had made for her. Berry placed the

finished necklace around her neck. She proudly spread her pink wings as she showed off her newest creation.

"Berry, Heart Day is coming up," Raina said gently. After she put the cap on the syrup bottle, she looked up at her friend. "Everyone in Sugar Valley is busy making candy hearts. And you're stringing round chews! You don't want to disappoint Princess Lolli, do you?"

Berry dragged her foot along the ground. There was a layer of powdered sugar that had fallen during the evening. It was a cold winter's day in Sugar Valley. The cool winds were blowing, and there was a chill in the air. "Sweet strawberries!" Berry exclaimed. "I would never want to upset Princess Lolli!"

Princess Lolli was the ruling fairy princess of Candy Kingdom. She was a caring and gentle fairy, and always treated the fairies very well. All the fairies loved her and wanted to please her. The sweet princess's favorite shape was a heart, so every fairy in the kingdom made special candy hearts from flavors found all over Sugar Valley. There were chocolate, gummy, mint, caramel, and fruit heart candies for Princess Lolli and the fairies to enjoy. Heart Day was a happy day, filled with good cheer—and delicious candy.

"I still have time to make something for Princess Lolli," Berry said. "Last year she loved my red fruit hearts, remember? I put a fruit surprise in each one and sprinkled them with red sugar."

Raina nodded. "Yes, and you spent weeks making those. Don't forget that Heart Day is next week."

"I will start on something today," Berry declared.

At that moment another Fruit Fairy flew up to the friends. Berry had just met her the other day. Her name was Fruli, and she was new to Sugar Valley. She had long blond hair, and today she was wearing the most beautiful dress

Berry had ever seen. There were tiny purple and pink candies sewn along the collar and cuffs that sparkled in the sun. Over her dress was a soft cape made of pink-and-white cotton candy. The fairy soared down next to them with her pale pink wings.

"Hi," Raina said. "You must be new here."

"This is Fruli," Berry said, introducing Raina to the newest Fruit Fairy. "She's from Meringue Island."

"Welcome to Sugar Valley," Raina said. "I've never been to Meringue Island, but I've read about the place. There's a story in the Fairy Code Book about the majestic Meringue Mountains. I've heard the island is beautiful and is the center of fashion." She smiled at Berry. "Berry loves fashion too."

Berry blushed. "Raina loves to read," she quickly explained. "She's memorized the Fairy Code Book."

Raina laughed. "Well, I do like to read. What about you, Fruli?"

"Yes, I like to read," she said very softly. She looked down at her white boots. Her response was so quiet that Berry and Raina could barely hear her.

"I love your cape," Raina said tentatively, eyeing the fabric and design. "Is that from Meringue Island?"

Fruli nodded. "Yes," she said. She didn't raise her eyes from the ground. "I'm sorry to interrupt."

Again, her voice was so low and soft, Berry and Raina could barely hear her.

"I just came to collect a couple of fruit chews for Princess Lolli," Fruli said.

"Well, you came to the right place," Raina said, smiling. She gave Berry a little push forward. She wondered why her friend was being so quiet around this new fairy. Usually, Berry was very outgoing and not shy at all. "Berry grows the best fruit chews on this side of the Frosted Mountains." She put her arm around her friend.

"Raina," Berry mumbled, feeling embarrassed. She smoothed her dress with her hands and noticed a big cherry syrup stain on the front.

Oh no, Berry thought. *What a big mess! Fruli has the nicest clothes. And look at me!*

"These chews?" Fruli asked, pointing.

"Yes," Berry said. "Please take anything you want."

Fruli took a few candies and put them in a white chocolate weave bag. "Thank you," she said.

Before Berry or Raina could say a word, she flew off.

"She was so shy!" Raina exclaimed.

"Did you see her clothes?" Berry asked. "She has the nicest outfits. I have *got* to get moving on making a new dress for Heart Day."

"Berry—," Raina started to say.

"I know," Berry said, holding up her hand. "I will make the heart candies, but I also need to find something new to wear to Candy Castle for Heart Day."

Berry flew off in a hurry, leaving Raina standing in Fruit Chew Meadow alone. Raina was worried. When Berry got an idea stuck in her head, sometimes things got a little sticky.

CHAPTER 2

Wild Cherry

Berry sat in front of two large pieces of fruit-dyed fabric. Bright pinks and reds were swirled around the material in large circles. Berry had been saving the material for something special, and a new outfit for Heart Day was the perfect occasion!

For a week she had tried drawing designs

for a new dress. Normally, designing a dress was fun and exciting for her. But this time nothing seemed right. To make things a little more sour, none of her friends understood her passion for fashion. Raina kept asking about heart candies, and her other friends did not seem interested in her dress designs. Berry sighed as she picked up the chalk to sketch out the dress form.

"I wish I could go to Meringue Island," she mumbled to herself. Even though the material in her hand was silky smooth, she was still feeling unsure. If only she could fly to the small, exclusive Meringue Island, she could buy a bunch of stylish new outfits. Meringue Island was known for high fashion and tons of cool accessories. Fruli probably thought all the fairies in Sugar Valley dressed terribly. Berry looked down at her red shiny dress. She used to love this one, but after seeing Fruli's dresses, she felt sloppy and very plain.

Berry didn't want to think about the beautiful dress that Fruli would be wearing on Heart Day. Thinking of what Fruli would wear made her face scrunch up like she had eaten a sour lemon ball.

I'll show her that Sugar Valley fairies know fashion and accessories too! Berry thought. She smoothed out the fabric and took out her scissors.

Her new dress was going to be the nicest one she'd ever made!

With thin caramel thread, Berry skillfully sewed up the dress. For extra sparkle, she added some of her new fruit chews around the collar.

She stood back and admired the dress. A smile spread across her face.

"Straight from the runways of Meringue Island," she said, pretending to be an announcer. "We are proud to carry the designs of Berry the Fruit Fairy!"

Berry slipped into the dress and spun around. Giggling, she felt so happy and glamorous. All her hard work had paid off.

Looking up at the sky, Berry noted the sun getting closer to the Frosted Mountains. Once the sun hit the top, Sun Dip would begin. At the end of the day her fairy friends gathered on the shores of Red Licorice Lake. They shared stories and snacked on candy. Usually, Berry was the last fairy to arrive.

Maybe today I'll surprise them, she thought. *I can be the first one there!*

She checked herself in the mirror and then flew out over the valley to Red Licorice Lake.

As she flew, Berry wished she had candy hearts for Princess Lolli. If the candies were finished, she'd have more time to make accessories for her new outfit. Berry smiled to herself. After all, accessories were the key to fashion! Maybe she could add a shawl, or even a cape? She had read all the fashion magazines and flipped through this season's catalogs. She could come up with something fabulous!

Seeing the tall spirals of Candy Castle off in the distance made Berry's heart sink. She realized she couldn't go to Heart Day empty-handed! She desperately needed a heart-shaped candy for the fairy princess.

Just then something red caught her eye. Down by the shores of Chocolate River there was something red and shiny glistening in the sun. Curious, Berry flew down to check out what was there. As she got closer, she saw that there was a small vine growing in the brown sugar sand.

"How odd," Berry said. Usually, there were some chocolate flowers growing there, but this vine looked different. She peered down closely at the plant. Berry couldn't believe her eyes! On the vine were tiny red hearts!

"Licking lollipops!" she cried out.

She reached down and plucked one of the hearts off the tiny vine.

Berry couldn't believe her luck. She was just wishing for candy hearts, and then they appeared!

These must be magic hearts, she thought.

Holding the heart in her hand, Berry examined the tiny candy. The rosy red color made her believe that these were cherry flavored. A bonus that cherry was one of Princess Lolli's favorite flavors. Carefully, Berry picked the hearts off the vine and placed them in her basket. Now she had something for Heart Day—and had time to finish her outfit!

After her basket was full, Berry flew over to Red Licorice Lake. It was the perfect day for her to be early for Sun Dip. She had lots to share with her friends today. She had news of her latest dress design, and magic heart candies for Princess Lolli. Maybe today wasn't so sour after all! Sweet wild cherry magic hearts just saved the day.

CHAPTER 3

Sweet Hearts

Berry spread her blanket on the red sugar sand and waited for her friends to arrive. The sun was just hitting the white tips of the mountains, and she knew that soon her friends would be there.

Dash the Mint Fairy was the first to arrive. Dash was the smallest Mint Fairy in the kingdom, but she had the biggest appetite!

"Berry, what are you doing here so early?" Dash cried as she swept down to the ground. She eyed Berry's new outfit. "You look fantastic. Is that a new dress?"

Smiling, Berry nodded. "I just made it!" she exclaimed.

"*So mint!*" Dash said. "I love the colors."

Cocoa the Chocolate Fairy and Melli the Caramel Fairy flew up next.

"Is this a special Sun Dip?" Melli asked. She looked Berry up and down. "You are wearing such a fancy dress."

"Hot chocolate! Where did you get that?" Cocoa asked, amazed. "It's fabulous."

Berry was enjoying all her friends' reactions to her new outfit. She stood up and spun in a circle. "It is pretty, don't you think?"

"I do," Melli said. "But I didn't get a sugar fly message about dressing up for tonight."

Berry laughed. "I just wanted to show you all my new outfit for Heart Day," she said.

"Yum!" Dash cheered. "I can't wait for Heart Day. I made the most delicious mint hearts, and Cocoa has promised to dip them in dark chocolate for me."

"That's right," Cocoa added. "Mint and chocolate hearts are an excellent combination." The two friends high-fived.

Dash turned to Melli. She knew that Melli and Cocoa often worked together, but this year Melli wanted to work on her own heart candies. "What did you make?"

A smile appeared on Melli's face. She dipped

her hand in her basket and pulled out a delicate heart.

"Is that caramel?" Dash asked, coming closer. She looked at the fragile heart in Melli's hand. The dark caramel looked like fine thread, but the candy was hard and didn't break when she touched it.

"That looks like imported lace!" Berry said. She leaned in to get a better look. "Melli, that is beautiful work."

"How long did that take you to make?" Dash asked.

Cocoa put her arm around Melli. "I told you these hearts were truly special," she told her.

Melli grinned. "Thank you," she said. "I've been working on these candies for weeks. I just hope Princess Lolli likes them."

"She's going to love those hearts," Dash told her. Then she licked her lips. "Maybe I should just try one to make sure they taste okay?"

"Dash!" Melli scolded. But then she started to laugh. "I knew you'd say that, so I brought some extra for tonight."

Dash's face brightened. "Ah, you are a good friend, Melli," she replied. Then she took a bite of the caramel heart. "Sweetheart, that is a *sweet heart*!" she said, laughing.

"Thank you," Melli said, and blushed.

"Wow, Berry!" Raina cried as she swooped down to her friends. "You have been working hard." She settled herself down on the blanket that Berry had spread out for the fairies. "The dress is beautiful. A true original."

Berry was bursting with pride.

"If you had time to make that dress, you must have finished your candy, right?" Raina asked.

Berry looked over at Raina. She had expected that Raina would say something like that. And she was ready! "Actually, I do have my heart candy," she replied. She placed her basket of tiny red hearts in the center of her blanket. Though she had not worked as hard on her candy as Melli, Berry was still excited to show off the new candy.

The fairies all moved closer to the basket.

"*So mint*!" Dash shouted. "Berry, you *do* have hearts for Princess Lolli!" She turned to look at Raina. "And you were worried about Berry. See, I told you she'd come through."

Berry hugged Dash. "Thanks, Dash," she said.

"You managed to make a dress and these

candies?" Melli asked. She peered into the basket. "That's very impressive, Berry."

Cocoa shook her head. "It takes me weeks to get chocolate hearts right," she said. "Hearts are the hardest shapes to make!"

"Well," Berry said. She was about to confess that she had found the candy, but then she held back.

Raina fluttered her wings. She peered down at the red candies. "There's something very familiar about these hearts," she said. She took the Fairy Code Book out of her bag. She placed the thick volume on the ground and quickly flipped through the pages. "I know I've seen those candies before." She didn't look up at her friends. She continued to thumb through the pages.

Dash reached over to the basket. "What flavor are they, Berry?"

"Cherry, of course," Berry stated proudly. "Princess Lolli's favorite flavor!"

Dash popped a heart in her mouth. Her blue eyes grew wide, and her wings flapped so fast she shot straight up in the air. "Holy peppermint!" she cried.

"What's wrong?" Cocoa exclaimed, reaching up to grab Dash. "Are you all right?"

"Those are not sweet hearts!" she said, scrunching up her face. "Those are sour wild cherry hearts!"

All the fairies gasped. Berry's hands flew to her mouth. Her not-so-sweet hearts had suddenly made Sun Dip very sour.

4

Sour Surprise

Berry shuddered. She felt awful about lying to her friends. She didn't know much about sour candy. She only knew that some was grown in Sour Orchard. While many fairies enjoyed the sweet-and-sour crops from the orchard at the far end of Sugar Valley, Berry did not. She preferred the sweet, fruity flavors of her own candy.

"Are you okay?" Berry asked Dash. She went over to her and put her hand on her friend's back. Dash's silver wings fluttered and brushed Berry's hand.

"Yes," Dash said. "I'm fine. I like those sour candies." She licked her fingers.

"Leave it to Dash to like just about any candy!" Cocoa said, giggling. "Even the most sour."

Dash shrugged her shoulders and looked over at Berry. "I just wasn't expecting that from a candy *you* grew," she said. "Those hearts looked so sweet and delicious."

Berry hung her head. "Well, I didn't grow these," she admitted, looking down at the ground. "I picked them from the bank of Chocolate River. They were beautiful—and heart-shaped."

"So you have no idea where these came from?" Melli asked. Her hand flew to her gaping mouth. "You don't know what these candies are made of?"

"And you didn't even test them first?" Cocoa added, amazed. "What happens if the hearts are poisonous or something horrible!"

"Cocoa!" Melli said. She never liked when her friends argued. She could tell that Cocoa's comment was making Berry upset. She turned her attention to Dash. "She looks the same. Are you feeling okay?"

"Stop looking at me like that!" Dash cried. "The hearts were good." She reached out toward Berry's basket.

"Dash!" all the fairies said at the same time. Berry grabbed her basket away.

"Cool down," Dash said. She sat on the ground next to Raina.

Suddenly Raina gasped. While her friends had been talking, she had been carefully reading the Fairy Code Book. "I knew those heart candies looked familiar," she said. She pointed to a picture at the bottom of the page. "Look here," she instructed.

The fairy friends all leaned over the book. There was a picture of the heart candies. And next to the picture was a drawing of Lemona, a Sour Orchard Fairy.

"Are they dangerous?" Cocoa asked.

"Don't be so dark," Melli said. She kneeled down closer to the book.

"Maybe they are magic because they simply

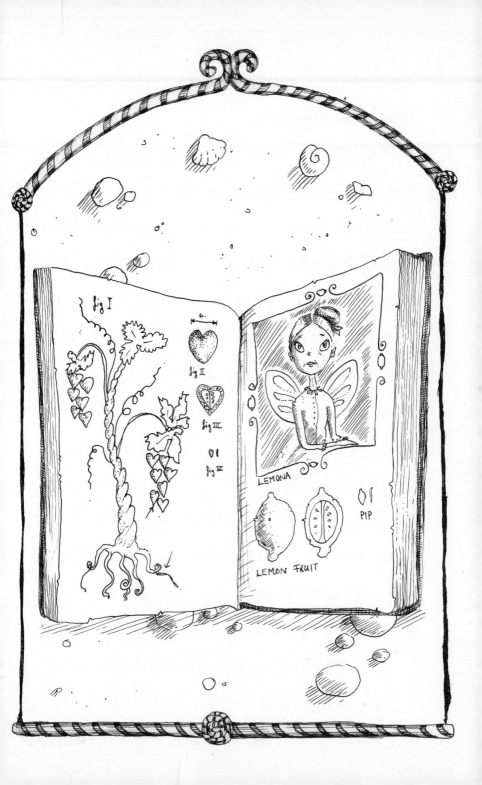

fig I

a.

fig II

fig III

fig III

LEMONA

LEMON FRUIT

PIP

appear when someone wishes for heart candies?" Berry said hopefully.

"Or maybe the hearts will make me fly faster down the mountain on my sled!" Dash exclaimed. She flew up in the air and did a high dive back down to the ground. "Wouldn't that be *so mint*?"

Berry knew that speeding down the Frosted Mountain trails was one of Dash's favorite things to do. Nothing would make her Mint Fairy friend happier than being the fastest fairy in the valley. She was already the smallest—and one of the fastest. While Dash flew in circles up in the air, Berry studied the Fairy Code Book. Her eyes grew wide as she read the rest of the information. She peered back up at Dash.

Sweet syrup! she thought. *What a sticky mess!*

Why hadn't she tested the candies? How could she have been so lazy? One of the first rules of making candy was that every fairy had to know the source of the ingredients. Berry's wings drooped lower to the ground as she read more about the magic hearts.

Dash came down and stood next to Berry's blanket. Berry wanted to tell her how sorry she was for what she had done. She had never meant to hurt Dash. She turned to her friend. But when Berry saw what was in front of her, she was speechless. Her mouth gaped open, and her eyes didn't budge from the sight in front of her.

"Why is everyone looking at me like that?" Dash asked. She saw the worried expressions on the faces in front of her.

The Fairy Code Book had used the words "might happen" to describe the effects of the candy. But something was *definitely* happening to Dash!

Dash's skin was bright yellow!

CHAPTER

5

A Big Heart

"Oh, Dash!" Berry cried out. She couldn't bear to see her friend a bright yellow color!

It was not often that fairies changed colors. Berry could think of one other time that had happened. A few years ago many of the fairies got the sugar flu. The virus was awful. Fairies couldn't fly or make any candy, and several fairies turned scarlet from the high fever. Princess Lolli set up stations in the castle for the sick fairies. Luckily, Berry, Melli, and Cocoa hadn't gotten the flu. But Dash and Raina had. Berry sighed. At least they were able to take medicine and get better. There were no viruses or germs to blame here.

This was all Berry's fault.

No one said anything. Dash fluttered her wings.

"Why is everyone staring at me?" she snapped.

"Well, she's certainly acting like the same old Dash," Cocoa said, watching the Mint Fairy.

"She doesn't look affected at all," Melli added. She shook her head in disbelief. "Except for the fact that she is now yellow."

"Yellow?" Dash screeched. "I'm yellow? As in

lemon frosting and lemon drops?" She looked down at her body and screamed.

Berry reached into her bag and gave Dash a small compact mirror. "Lemon yellow," Berry said sadly. "Take a look in the mirror. You'll see the color is all over your face."

Dash opened the candy-jeweled case and peered into the mirror. "A yellow Mint Fairy?" she cried. She snapped the mirror shut. Panicked, Dash grabbed Raina's hand. "Please tell me this will go away." When there was no reply from Raina, Dash took a deep breath. "Well, is there any medicine I can take? There must be something to make this go away, right?" She examined her yellow arms and hands.

Raina flipped through some more pages of the Fairy Code Book. "I can't find anything

more here in the book," she said. "It's odd. The book only mentions a slight change of coloring. I wonder why the bright yellow?"

"If Raina doesn't know the answer, this must be bad," Cocoa whispered to Melli.

"There is no medicine for magic spells," Melli said. "Oh, Dash . . ."

"Melli is right," Raina added. "We'll need to figure out the magic before you can get better."

"Why yellow?" Dash balked. "Blech!"

"There's only one way to fix this," Berry said. She stood up. "I have to go ask Lemona about her candy. If she's the fairy who made the candy, she'll know the answer to this riddle."

"What?" Dash said. "You, Berry the sweet and beautiful Fruit Fairy, want to venture into Sour Orchard?"

Dash might have been mocking Berry, but there was truth to what she was saying. Berry enjoyed fine fashions and sparkly accessories and was not one for flying out of her comfortable sweet spots.

"What if Lemona is as sour as her candy?" Melli asked.

"Oh, how awful," Cocoa said. "Do you think she could be like Mogu?"

"Mogu is a salty old troll who lives in Black Licorice Swamp," Raina said, shaking her head. "Lemona is one of us, a Candy Fairy."

"A Candy Fairy who lives in Sour Orchard," Melli mumbled.

Dash flew around in circles. "This color can't last, can it?" she asked. When no one answered, Dash landed and hung her head.

"Holy peppermint," she whispered. "I'll be the joke of Sugar Valley."

Berry took Dash's hand. "Don't get upset, Dash," she said. "I am going to find a way to help you. I promise."

"You'd really go to Sour Orchard for me?" Dash asked. She peered up at Berry.

"I should never have neglected my candy duties," Berry admitted. She folded her knees up to her chest. "If I hadn't been so concerned about making a new dress, then I would have made time to grow my own candy hearts for Heart Day." She gazed at Dash. "And I should have told the truth about those heart candies. Will you forgive me?"

"I'm not mad," Dash said. "I understand." She stuck her hand in her backpack. "Here, take these peppermint candies. It's getting dark and you might need light in Sour Orchard."

"Thank you," Berry told her. Dash might have been small, but she had the biggest heart of all. "I am truly sorry."

Suddenly Raina shot up from her spot on the blanket. "Oh, I found something more here," she said. She pointed to a section in the Fairy Code Book.

"I don't think I've ever been so grateful for that book," Dash said. She moved closer to Raina.

"When visiting Sour Orchard," Raina began to read, "you should bring a gift to a Sour Orchard Fairy. Sour Orchard Fairies are fond of fresh fruit blossoms."

Berry smiled. "I know where to get some

fresh and delicious orange blossoms!"

Even though it was winter in Sugar Valley, the orange trees were blossoming. The magic orange trees produced tangy and sweet candy fruit all year. Fruit Fairies took the oranges and dipped the slices into chocolate or made sweet fruit nectar for candies throughout the valley. Just that morning Berry had flown by the orange trees along the edge of Fruit Chew Meadow. Their sweet citrus smell always made her smile. It seemed even Sour Orchard Fairies enjoyed the fresh scents and tastes of the blossoms.

"Going to Sour Orchard with something to make Lemona happy will make the journey easier," Berry said.

"I'll go with you," Raina told her.

"You will?" Berry asked. "I thought you were angry at me."

Raina closed her book and slipped it back into her backpack. "I can see you are very sorry," she said. "And I don't want you to go by yourself. It's always better to fly with a friend."

Feeling overwhelmed, Berry reached out to hug her friend. "You are a good friend, Raina. Thank you."

"Melli and I will stay with Dash," Cocoa said. "I have some chocolate dots here that should keep her happy for a while."

"Thanks," Dash said. "But I don't really feel like eating right now."

Hearing Dash refuse candy made Berry move a little faster. Dash never declined a piece of candy!

"We'll go now," Berry told her. "We'll be back before bedtime. I promise you won't go to sleep a yellow Mint Fairy." She gave Dash a big hug and then waved to Melli and Cocoa. She was glad they'd be with Dash to look after her.

Together, Berry and Raina flew off toward Fruit Chew Meadow to gather orange blossoms for Lemona. Berry hoped with all her heart that the meeting would go well—and that Lemona could help get Dash back to normal. Otherwise, Heart Day was not going to be a happy day.

Spooky Meadow

When Berry and Raina arrived at Fruit
Chew Meadow, the sun had just slid to the
other side of the Frosted Mountains. Berry flew
over to the row of orange trees along the side
of the meadow. The sweet citrus scent smelled
delicious. Being in the meadow made Berry feel
safe and relaxed. But she didn't have time to

rest! If they wanted to talk to Lemona before the evening stars came out, she and Raina would have to hurry.

"How can anyone be mean *and* like orange blossoms?" Berry asked Raina. She put her nose close to the beautiful orange flower.

"Mmmm," Raina said. She flew over to Berry and smelled the flower candy. "I know what you mean. Sure as sugar, these do smell sweet." She thought for a moment and then looked up at Berry. "Maybe Sour Orchard Fairies aren't as sour as their candy. You know in the Fairy Code Book there is no mention of what the Sour Orchard Fairies are like—just the kind of candy they grow."

Berry raised her eyebrows. "Have you ever met a Sour Orchard Fairy?" she asked Raina.

"No," Raina said slowly. "I've only seen one once, at Candy Castle last year at Candy Fair. She had green wings and a light green dress. I think she brought sour apple suckers to the castle."

Berry nodded. She remembered the fair last year, when all the fairies in the valley came to the summer celebration in the Royal Gardens. There were a few Sour Orchard Fairies there, but Berry hadn't talked to them. "They always look so . . ." She searched for the right word.

"Sour?" Raina asked, giggling. "I guess we don't really know, if we've never spoken to them." She helped Berry pick a few more blossoms from the tree. "Maybe we'll find out that Lemona is really a sweet fairy."

Berry put a bunch of the fragrant blossoms

in her basket. "Or maybe the Fairy Code Book suggests taking the blossoms to make sure the fairies don't get sour when a visitor comes." Her wings shook as she imagined having to face a sour fairy.

"Oh, Berry, your dress!" Raina cried.

Looking down, Berry saw orange stains on her new dress. "Oh, it's just as well," she said. "This dress wasn't really working for me anyway."

"Wait, did you just hear something rustling over there?" Raina asked, pointing to the ground. She squinted in the dark. "I don't like being here after Sun Dip."

"That must have been the wind," Berry told her. She flew down to the ground and looked around the trunk of the tree. "No one's here."

"Then where is that light coming from?" Raina asked, quivering. There was an eerie green glow getting closer and closer to the orange tree.

Berry turned around. Out of the darkness a fairy appeared.

"Aaaaah!" Berry and Raina screamed.

"Sorry," Fruli answered. "I didn't mean to scare you." She pointed her glowing peppermint candy at the ground. "I didn't think anyone would be here now," she said very softly.

Raina gasped. "Oh, Fruli!" she exclaimed. "You scared the sugar out of me!" Her hand flew to her chest. Her heart was beating so fast she could hardly breathe. "What are you doing here?"

Fruli's wings began to beat even faster. "I . . . I . . . I like to come here when the day is over and smell the orange blossoms. The sweet smell

helps me to sleep. There are orange trees like this on Meringue Island, and the smell reminds me of home."

Berry was trying to get Raina's attention. She didn't want her mentioning to Fruli what they were doing. All Berry needed was for Fruli to know that she had picked sour wild cherry hearts—and given them to one of her best friends. Worse yet, she couldn't let her know that Dash was yellow because of her!

"We have to get going," Berry said quickly. She grabbed a shawl from her bag and covered her stained dress. Then she pulled on Raina's hand and took her to the other side of the meadow.

"Berry!" Raina cried. "We didn't even good-bye. Why are you acting so rude?"

"Did you forget about Dash? She's yel

I'm just trying to get to Lemona as soon as possible," Berry explained.

"Fruli seems so nice," Raina said, shaking her head. "You could have at least asked her what she did for Sun Dip. Maybe she'd want to hang out with us. She seemed homesick."

"She's too fancy. She wouldn't want to hang out with us," Berry said. "Did you see her dress?" She sighed wistfully. "She has the most glamorous clothes. She'd never want to have Sun Dip with us. She'd want to be up at the castle or with the older Fruit Fairies."

Raina eyed her friend. "Maybe, but maybe not. Have you ever asked her?"

"Why are you on her side?" Berry snapped.

"I'm not," Raina said. "I just think you could have been a little sweeter to Fruli."

Berry huffed and rolled her eyes. "Raina, she's not some lost gummy cub." She packed up the orange blossoms and looked up at Raina. "What? I'm just saying that she's fine and we're late. Come on!"

Raina shook her head. When Berry had a mission, she was focused. She knew her Fruit Fairy friend could be stubborn. She was all juiced up. "Let's get going," Raina said. "I think we have enough orange blossoms for Lemona now."

Taking flight, Berry soared through the air. She had never ventured past Chocolate River to Sour Orchard. Being there at night made things seem even spookier. She hoped with all her heart that Lemona would tell them how they could help Dash. As Berry glided over the valley with

Raina, she held tightly to her basket of orange blossoms. If the sweet smell didn't sway the sour fairy, she hoped she and Raina could. She just had to have the answer that would help Dash. Berry's heart was breaking just thinking about Dash's being yellow. This plan had to work!

CHAPTER 7

Brave Hearts

Sour Orchard was bursting with lemon, lime, cherry, apple, and orange trees. But these trees were different from the ones Berry and Raina were used to seeing in Fruit Chew Meadow and Gummy Forest. These trees grew in the tangy sugar crystals of Sour Orchard. Thick tree trunks held up heavy branches filled with sweet and sour fruits.

Berry peered down at the orchard. "I wish it wasn't so dark," she said.

"I know," Raina said. "It's a little spooky here. But at least there's some moonlight."

"Let's fly lower so we can see better," Berry called. The orchard was much larger than Berry thought it would be. Even in the dim light, she could see that there were several rows of trees.

As she flew Berry looked at all the fruits on the trees. The thought of eating those sour candies made her mouth water. There were trees dripping with bunches of sour candy suckers and fruits.

Berry knew Fruit Chew Meadow so well that even in the dark she could find her way, but this place was different. The trees looked different and the smells were not the same.

"Thanks for coming with me," Berry whispered to Raina. She grabbed her hand. "I'm sorry I snapped at you before."

"It's okay," Raina said. "Besides, I wouldn't have let you come alone."

"You are a good friend," Berry told her. She squeezed her friend's hand tighter.

Berry spotted a familiar vine growing on a tree deep in the orchard. She pulled Raina along as she swooped down to look.

"Raina!" she exclaimed. "This is the same vine that was growing by Chocolate River! This is the magic heart vine!"

Berry landed next to the vine, and Raina followed. "Sure as sugar!" she said. "I knew those candies were magic hearts." She looked around. "Lemona must live somewhere around here."

Taking a walk around a lemon tree, Berry searched for a sign of the Sour Fairy. Her red boots crunched on the sour sugar coating the ground. "What does the Fairy Code Book say? What type of home does she have?"

"Look!" Raina exclaimed. She pointed to a sign on a lemon tree a few feet away. A small piece of fruit leather had "Lemona" etched on it. "She must live over there."

Lemona's house! Berry's heart began to race. She wasn't sure what to say to the fairy, but she knew she had to talk to her. She had to confess that she had given the candy to her friend without testing it first. As hard as that would be, Berry knew she had to find out the truth about the candy. And the secret of the magic hearts.

Before they stepped closer to the tree, a small sugar fly flew up to Berry. The messenger buzzed around her ears.

"You have a message for me?" Berry asked.

The sugar fly nodded and handed her the note. Immediately, Berry saw that the note was from Melli. Her breath caught in her chest and she gasped. "Oh, Raina! What if something horrible has happened?" she cried. Berry's wings started to flutter and she flew up in the air. "I will never forgive myself if something has happened to Dash. What was I thinking, giving out candy that I didn't know about!"

Raina touched Berry's arm. "Let's see what

the note says. We don't know what this is about yet."

Berry's hand was shaking. "I can't," she said, handing the note to Raina. "Would you please read this for me? I can't bear to read any more sour news today."

"Maybe the news isn't bad," Raina said. She tried to smile encouragingly at her friend.

"Please read it," Berry pleaded.

Raina opened the letter. "Dash is fine," she read. "But she is now orange! Please hurry and send along any information that you get." Raina looked up from the note. "Oh, sugar," she said. "This is worse than I thought."

Berry's eyes grew wide. "What do you mean?" she gasped.

"Well, she's turning more than one color,"

Raina said. "That's not a good sign."

Berry turned to see the sugar fly. He was waiting for a return note. Quickly, Berry scribbled a message back to her friends. "We'll soon be on our way with help," she said as she wrote the note. "Hold on. We've just arrived at the orchard." She folded up the note and handed it to the sugar fly. "Please give this to Melli or Cocoa," she instructed the sugar fly.

"Are you all right?" Raina asked, looking at Berry.

Suddenly Berry was juiced up. Dash needed her help, and she was going to get her out of this sour mess. She wasn't going to be afraid. She was simply going to ask Lemona what was in her candy and how to help get Dash back to normal.

"Let's not dip our wings in syrup yet!" Berry said. She put her hands on her hips, charged with confidence. "We're here, aren't we? We need to have brave hearts!"

Raina grinned. Her spunky friend was back! And just in time. If they were going to talk to Lemona, they needed to be brave and confident.

"Lemona will help us," Berry said. With a burst of hope, she walked toward Lemona's tree.

Just then a cloud passed over the full moon, blocking the bright moonlight for a brief moment. Berry and Raina stood still in the middle of Sour Orchard, unsure of what to do. They were so close to Lemona's tree, but they couldn't see a thing!

CHAPTER 8

Sweet Sours

Licking lollipops!" Berry cried. "It's too dark!" How could they talk to Lemona if they couldn't find her front door?

"Wait," Raina said. "I have those peppermint candies that Dash gave us before we left." She dug around into her bag and pulled out a bright candy.

Berry smiled. "When we get back, we'll have to thank Dash for giving those to us," she said.

In the pale green light of the glowing peppermint, the two fairies were able to find their way to Lemona's tree.

Berry paused before knocking on the door. There was a strong scent of lemon in the air, and Berry turned to Raina. "Ready?" she asked.

"If you are," the Gummy Fairy said, trying to sound brave.

Berry took a deep breath and knocked on the door. The door opened, and there stood a small, older fairy.

"Hello," the fairy said. She peered over her glasses to look at Berry and Raina. "Two young fairies at my door past Sun Dip?" she asked. "What brings you two here?"

"We've come for some help," Berry said bravely.

The older fairy nodded, and opened her door wider to invite them in. Her pale yellow hair was pulled back in a tight bun, and her wings and her dress were both yellow. "Come in," she said kindly.

Berry and Raina walked into the fairy's house. Berry eyed Lemona. Her yellow dress was simple and neat, and her wings were gold. She had large almond-shaped eyes that were a bright green, complementing her blond hair. She didn't look sour and mean, but Berry couldn't be so sure.

Lemona strode over to a chair near the fireplace. There was a large yellow cauldron on the fire and a plate of lemon drop candies

on a table. She stirred the pot and dropped a few lemon candies in. A poof of smoke flew from the pot. Lemona sat down in her chair and waved to Berry and Raina to have a seat on a small couch.

"What are you cooking?" Raina asked. She smelled the air. "Whatever it is, it smells delicious."

"It's a lemon broth for the candy hearts I am making," she said. She settled herself in her chair. "I'm getting too old for this!" she exclaimed as she leaned back into the chair. "Heart Day always sneaks up on me and I wind up rushing."

Berry nodded. She knew exactly how Lemona felt!

"Actually, that is why we're here," Berry said. She took a deep breath and told Lemona her story. As she sat by the fire she was amazed how easy it was to talk to Lemona. Berry wound up telling her all about Fruli and how she wanted to make a new dress. Then she explained how she had found the magic hearts.

"All the way by Chocolate River?" Lemona remarked. "My sweet sours, I have never heard of the wind carrying the seeds that far!"

"You mean this has happened before?" Raina asked. She sat on the edge of her seat, listening. This should be entered in the Fairy Code Book!

The older fairy nodded. "Yes, sometimes the strong winter winds make the seeds take flight." She reached over to stir the pot. "What did you do with the candy?"

Berry looked down at her hands in her lap. "Well, I let my friend Dash the Mint Fairy eat one," Berry told Lemona. "I know that I shouldn't have done that." She looked up at Lemona. "Now Dash is turning colors. She was yellow and now she's orange!"

Lemona shook her head. "I'm sorry to hear that," she said. "You know that candy doesn't always look the way it tastes."

"Yes, ma'am," Berry said. She kept her eyes on the ground. She was more embarrassed than ever. That is one of the first rules of candy making.

Lemona heaved herself out of her chair and walked over to the pantry. She opened up the cupboard and took out a jar. Inside were brightly colored crystal sugars, and Lemona poured a stream into the pot. "And how is Dash feeling?" she asked.

"She seems to be fine," Berry told her. "Except

her color is off. She doesn't want to be a yellow or orange Mint Fairy."

"I understand," Lemona said.

Berry couldn't believe how kind Lemona was being. When she sat and talked to the young fairies, she didn't have a sour face at all! In fact, Lemona was being so sweet that Berry started to relax.

"Those wild flavors are a bit tricky at times," Lemona finally said. She stood up to add a few more lemon drops in the cauldron.

"Can you help Dash?" Berry asked.

"I believe I know just the thing for your Mint Fairy friend," Lemona said thoughtfully. She pulled a book down from the shelf behind her.

Raina's eyes widened. She had never seen

that book before. She leaned over to get a closer look at *Sour Orchard, Volume III.*

"Will it say in there what to do?" Berry asked anxiously.

Lemona wrapped a yellow shawl around her arms carefully. "Let me just make sure," she said.

Berry glanced over at Raina. She hoped this trip to Sour Orchard would turn out to be worth their while. She couldn't bear to get another sugar fly message that Dash had turned yet another color!

Please, please, Berry wished as Lemona bent over the large book, *please find what you are looking for in there!*

CHAPTER

9

A Peppermint Plan

Berry and Raina sat on the edge of their seats as Lemona reviewed the large Sour Orchard history book. The two fairies watched as Lemona slowly turned the pages. She stopped once to take a sip from her yellow teacup. It was so hard to wait patiently as Lemona tried to find the answer to their question. This was worse than waiting for fruit-chew jewelry to dry!

Looking around the room, Berry noticed that Lemona had many pieces of art hanging in her home. Lemona reminded Berry of her great-aunt Razz. She was a wise and beloved Fruit Fairy. Razz had pieces of art hanging in her home too. Berry never would have imagined that she would feel so comfortable in a Sour Orchard Fairy's house! She couldn't wait to get back and tell Cocoa, Melli, and Dash. That is, if Lemona could solve Dash's dilemma.

Raina looked over at Berry and smiled.

Berry was so glad her good friend was with her. "I wouldn't have been able to do this without you," she whispered.

"Oh, sure you would have," Raina said,

swatting her hand. "But I am happy to be here now. And I think Lemona is going to be able to help us."

At that moment Lemona spoke up. "Oh, here it is!" she exclaimed. She took off her lemon-colored glasses and waved them in the air. "I knew it was in here somewhere."

"Oh, please tell us," Berry pleaded. "I want Dash to be back to her normal mint self."

"It's just as I had thought," Lemona said. She peered over at Berry. "This will take some work, and you'll have to act quickly."

"Anything for Dash!" Berry declared.

"Tell us what we need to do," Raina said.

Pointing to the open page, Lemona read the instructions. "You must gather leaves from Peppermint Grove," she said. "The leaves must be fresh from the vine, not from the ground." She gazed up at the two fairies.

Both Berry and Raina nodded.

"Fresh mint leaves," Berry repeated.

Lemona returned her attention to the book and continued to read. "Make a strong cup of peppermint tea," she instructed. "Eat three peppermint candies from the old mint tree in the northern part of Peppermint Grove, and get plenty of rest." Lemona looked up at the two young fairies. "If she does all that, in the morning she'll wake up her own self."

Berry popped off her seat. "Peppermint tea will cure her?" she asked.

Lemona nodded.

"You'd be surprised how many ailments are cured by peppermint tea!"

Raina stood up. "I know the tree you are talking about," she said. "We'll get those things to Dash straightaway."

"Thank you very much," Berry said to Lemona. "You have been so helpful." Then she paused for a moment. "Thank you for being so sweet to us."

The Sour Orchard Fairy threw her head back and laughed. "Oh, please," she said. "We all make mistakes. I hope you've learned that you can't assume a candy is a certain way because of its color and shape."

"Yes!" Berry exclaimed.

Sure as sugar, she thought. She would never again assume any candy would be a certain way.

She pulled off two candy jewels from her dress and handed them to Lemona. "I'd like to give you something."

"Did you make these?" Lemona asked. "They are beautiful."

"Thank you," Berry said, blushing. "I'd love for you to have them. They make neat hair clips," she added.

Lemona reached out and gave Berry a hug. And Berry gave the yellow fairy a tight squeeze back.

"We must get going," Berry said. "We've got to get Dash her tea."

"Yes, it's getting late," Raina added. "We should be going."

Lemona stood up and walked the fairies to the door. "Thank you for coming," she said. "And for the candy jewels."

"Thank you," Raina said. "It really was a pleasure to meet you. Will we see you at Heart Day?"

Lemona smiled. "Of course," she said. "I love Heart Day. I'll be there, and I'd love to see you and your Mint Fairy friend as well."

"Licking lollipops!" Berry said. "We all wouldn't miss it for the world."

For the first time since Dash had taken a bite of the magic heart candy, Berry had hope that everything could go back to normal. She may not have a new dress to wear to Heart Day, but maybe Dash would be back to herself for the celebration.

As fast as fairies can fly, Berry and Raina flew to Peppermint Grove and got the peppermint leaves for the tea and the three candies. Then they quickly flew to Red Licorice Lake, where they knew Melli, Cocoa, and Dash were waiting.

"They're back!" Cocoa cried when she spotted her friends in the air. "Did you find Lemona?"

"Was she sour like Mogu?" Melli asked. "Or did she agree to help you?"

Berry looked around. There were a few peppermints giving off a soft glow to light up the area. "Where's Dash?"

"I'm here," Dash said. Her voice was muffled.

"Where are you, Dash?" Berry asked. She looked to Melli and Cocoa. Both of her friends pointed to a stack of picked licorice stalks.

"She hasn't come out of there since she started to turn orange," Cocoa told her.

Berry knelt down and peered inside the nest of licorice. "Dash, can you come out? It's just us. Raina and I have something for you."

"Will it make me return to my normal color?" Dash asked. "I'm red now!"

Melli's hand flew to her mouth. "Hot caramel," she said. "This is getting serious."

"Don't worry," Berry said. "We found Lemona, and you just need to drink some peppermint tea and eat some peppermint candy."

"All things you love," Raina added. "And we picked everything fresh from the grove. Honest." She peered over Berry's shoulder to look into the licorice nest. "Fairy Code honor."

There was a bit of rustling, and a few licorice stalks shifted. Dash's head popped out. "No laughing!" she said, her hands covering her face.

"Oh, Dash," Berry said. "I don't care what color you are, you will always be my friend."

"But look at me!" Dash cried. "I'm red!"

Raina stepped forward. "But not for long, Dash." She handed her a candy teacup of peppermint tea, and the three peppermint candies. "Lemona said to have these and then get a good night's rest."

Dash took the tea and candy from Raina and gulped everything down. She sat down on the red sugar sand and peered up at her friends.

"Do I look any different?" she asked.

"Not yet," Berry said.

"You match the sand," Cocoa blurted out.

Melli shot Cocoa a stern look.

"But I'm sure you'll be feeling like yourself soon," Cocoa added quickly.

"Lemona was so sweet, Dash," Berry told her. "She looked up the problem in a book and was so willing to help. In the morning you'll be feeling minty fresh, sure as sugar!"

Dash pulled the hood of her sweater over her head. "I hope you're right," she said. "Otherwise, there is no way I'm going to Heart Day like this."

Berry's heart sank. Heart Day without Dash? That would be awful! This peppermint plan had to work.

10

True Hearts

Berry raced across Sugar Valley in the early morning light. She was rushing to get to Dash's house. She hoped that when Dash greeted her at the door, her friend would look like herself. She couldn't bear to see Dash red, pink, purple, or any other color!

The Royal Gardens were already set up for

the Heart Day celebration. From the sky above, Berry could see that the Castle Fairies were hard at work. There were small red and pink candy hearts draped from the tall sugar gates, and large heart-shaped candies hung from the royal candy trees. It was one gigantic heart fest!

Sighing, Berry hoped the day would go as she had planned. She wanted to be at the party with *all* her friends. She knew that if Dash wasn't herself, the proud Mint Fairy would not go to the castle party. And that would be all Berry's fault!

Berry raced up to Dash's door. She knocked several times. Berry was not known for her patience, and the Fruit Fairy couldn't wait a second longer at Dash's doorstep.

"I'm coming!" Dash finally cried from the

other side. As she opened the door, the bright morning light made her squint. She rubbed her eyes. "Berry?" she said. "What are you doing here so early?"

"I wanted to come see you first thing!" she blurted out. For the first time ever Berry was extremely early! She had jumped out of bed and quickly dressed. She wanted to be at Dash's side when she woke up.

"Holy peppermint," Dash said. "I don't think I've ever seen you anywhere so early!"

Berry didn't even respond. She pulled Dash out into the bright sunlight. She gasped and reached out to give Dash a hug. "You look like your old minty self!" she cried.

"Never underestimate the power of pepper-mint tea," Dash said, grinning. "I am feeling much better." She smiled up at Berry. "And looking much better too," she added. She rolled up her sleeves and grinned at her normal color. She was back!

"Oh, Dash," Berry gushed. "I am so glad! Sweet strawberries! This is going to be a great day!"

"But you didn't have a chance to make your heart candy or finish your new outfit," Dash said. She eyed Berry's dress. "And you're not even wearing the new dress you made."

"Don't make that sour face," Berry said, smiling. "That other dress was stained. Besides, I love this red dress. It's red for Heart Day!" She twirled around in front of Dash. "Look, I even added a sugar crystal heart here on the waistband." Berry leaned down and showed

Dash the sparkly heart she had sewn on. "I'm going to give Princess Lolli my heart-shaped fruit-chew barrettes."

"Princess Lolli will love those. And you always look fantastic," Dash said. "Even when you are rushed!" She turned back and called over her shoulder. "I'll be ready in a minty minute!"

Just as Dash ducked back behind her door, Melli, Raina, and Cocoa flew up. Each of them held their heart candies for Heart Day. Before they could say anything, Berry blurted out the good news about Dash.

"Dash is looking *so mint*!' Berry shouted. "It's truly a happy Heart Day after all."

"A day of hearts and true friendship," Raina cheered.

Berry nodded. "Thank you," she said.

"I've really learned my lesson. And I've been thinking . . ."

"Oh no," Cocoa said. "What are you up to now, Berry?"

Laughing, Berry walked over to Cocoa and gave her hand a squeeze. "I was just thinking that I haven't been very sweet to a new Fruit Fairy."

"You mean Fruli?" Raina asked.

"Who's Fruli?" Melli said.

Berry hung her head. "Fruli is from Meringue Island. She's new to Sugar Valley. Instead of trying to be nice to her, I've just been very jealous of her. And that's the ugliest and most sour way to be," she admitted.

"Is she going to be at Heart Day?" Melli asked.

"I hope so," Berry said. "I'd like you all to meet her."

Raina smiled at Berry. "You were thinking about what Lemona told you, huh?"

"Yes," Berry confessed. "I was thinking the same thing could be true about fairies, not just candies. I never took the time to get to know Fruli. Maybe she's different from what I thought."

"A perfect plan for Heart Day," Melli said.

"Yes, and the real meaning of Heart Day," Raina said.

"It's not just a party. It's a celebration of good friends," Cocoa chimed in.

"You can be sure as sugar it's a celebration!" Dash said as she zoomed out of her house. "Let's go have a heart feast!"

Together, the five fairies flew to the Royal

Gardens. There were already many fairies gathered in a line to see Princess Lolli. Lemona waved and winked at Berry when she saw her holding Dash's hand.

"Nice to see you all here," Lemona said as she flew by.

"Hello, Lemona!" Berry called out. She noticed that Lemona had put the candy jewels in her hair for the party.

"Was that a Sour Orchard Fairy?" Dash asked.

"Yes," Berry replied. "And one of the sweetest fairies you'll ever meet."

When the fairy friends joined the line to greet Princess Lolli, Berry spotted Fruli. She was dressed in a beautiful soft pink chiffon dress and was holding a cherry red heart-shaped box.

"Hi, Fruli," Berry called. "I'd like you to meet some of my friends." Berry introduced everyone and then smiled at Fruli. "And I want to apologize to you. I haven't been very nice. Please accept my apology."

A smile spread across Fruli's face. "Thank you," she said. She looked right at Berry as she spoke. "It's been hard being the new fairy. I would love to meet some new friends."

"And Heart Day is just the day for making new friends!" Princess Lolli said. She greeted the fairies and gave them each a hug. "Thank you all for coming and for these wonderful heart gifts." She looked over at Berry. "And I see you have found the true message of Heart Day already."

Berry beamed. "Sure as sugar!" she cried.

She looked around at her good friends, and her new friends. Meeting Lemona and Fruli had made this an extra-special Heart Day. No candy heart was sweeter than making new friends!

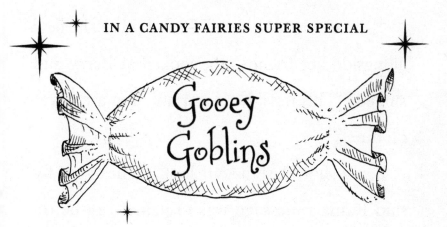

Gooey Goblins

Cocoa the Chocolate Fairy, Melli the Caramel Fairy, and Berry the Fruit Fairy soared over Chocolate River. A cool autumn breeze ruffled their wings, but they stayed their course. Nothing was going to stop them from heading to the far end of Gummy Forest.

"Look—there's Dash!" Cocoa called. As the

three fairy friends neared Peppermint Grove, they saw their tiny friend shooting up to meet them.

"You are right on time," Dash said as she flew alongside her friends. She looked at Berry and smiled. "This must be important. You are never on time!"

Berry shot Dash a sour look. "The sugar fly said Raina's message was urgent. I can be on time when I need to be!"

"And yet she still had time to put on her best sugar jewel necklace," Cocoa added with a sly grin.

"Just because I was rushing doesn't mean I have to look sloppy," Berry replied. Berry always liked to look her best and was usually sporting a new piece of jewelry that she made herself from sparkling sugar-coated fruit chews.

"What do you think this is all about?" Melli asked. She was worried about her friend Raina the Gummy Fairy. Usually Raina didn't overreact to situations. She was very calm and always followed the rules.

"Maybe she just couldn't find something in the Fairy Code Book and needs our help," Cocoa joked.

"No, there's definitely something strange blowing around the valley," Dash said. She looked back at her friends. "And no, it's not just the cold autumn wind," she added.

Melli had to agree with Dash. "This is the busiest time in Sugar Valley and we shouldn't be distracted from our work. Candy Corn Field is already full of tall stalks."

The four fairies flew in silence for a moment. They glided over Candy Castle and then they saw the tops of the Gummy trees.

"I can't wait to see Raina," Melli said. "I hope that she's all right."

"We just saw her yesterday," Berry told her. "Don't be so dramatic. I'm sure that she's fine."

Cocoa flew ahead and then called back over her shoulder, "I don't think that it's Raina that we need to be concerned about." She pointed to the south end of the forest. "Look at those trees!"

The four friends gasped as they saw the melted leaves of the gummy trees. Normally, the branches were filled with bright rainbow gummy fruits.

"No wonder she called us," Berry whispered.

"Let's go find her," Dash said.

The fairies flew deeper into the forest. There were puddles everywhere from the melted gummy candies.

"I never thought that I would say this," Dash said. "But Gummy Forest is a melted mess!" She stepped over a rainbow puddle. Even though Dash was the smallest of all the Candy Fairies, she was always hungry and was the most adventurous eater. If the melted gummies didn't appeal to even Dash, the fairies knew things were *really* bad.

"Sweet sugar!" Raina shouted when she saw her friends. "I'm so glad that you got here!"

"Oh, Raina," Melli said, rushing down to give her friend a hug. "What happened here?"

"I'm not really sure," Raina said, her voice full

of concern. "When I woke up this morning, the forest looked . . . melted!"

Cocoa, Berry, and Dash landed beside her. Their faces told Raina all she needed to know.

"It still looks awful here, doesn't it?" the Gummy Fairy asked. "The poor forest animals don't know what to make of all this. I tried my best to take away some of the melted candies and clean up some of the puddles, but that doesn't seem to be making a difference. The forest is still a mess."

"Are you okay?" Cocoa asked. She put her arm around Raina.

Raina sat down on a melted log on the ground. "I'm fine," she said with a heavy sigh. "I've been doing all sorts of research. And nothing seems to match up. All I know is that the forest animals and Gummy candies are all in danger."

"It's definitely eerie, not cheery, here," Berry muttered. "Are you sure this isn't some kind of spooky trick from Mogu?"

Raina shook her head. "I don't think so. This is really bad. Even for a tricky troll."

"I wouldn't put anything past Mogu," Cocoa said. "That old, salty troll is sour."

"Yes," Raina agreed. "But Mogu loves gummy candy. I can't see him wanting to ruin it."

The fairies all knew that Mogu lived in the Black Licorice Swamp and often came with his Chuchies to swipe candy from the Gummy Forest. The troll and his round little workers loved candy too much to spoil the crops.

Berry looked closely at the melted trees. "I think that you're right. These candies are ruined . . . even for a troll to eat."

"I told you something was going on," Dash mumbled.

Standing with her hands on her hips, Berry shook her head. "You're not saying what I think that you're saying, are you?" She smiled at Dash. "You've been reading too many Caramel Moon stories."

"Most of the stories are based on truth," Dash said. She loved to read all the spooky tales that fairies had spun about the full moon in the tenth month of the year. "Those aren't just ghost stories." Dash looked over at Melli and Raina. "Tell them!"

"Well, some of those stories are just meant to

entertain," Raina said. "But others are based on true occurrences."

Dash gloated for a minute, but then a melted candy snapped off its vine and fell on her head. She rubbed her forehead and looked to Raina. "What do you think this is all about?"

Raina plucked a droopy gummy branch off a tree. "Has anyone else seen anything strange going on in Sugar Valley?" She glanced over at Dash. "Or heard anything strange?"

"The Gummy flowers over by the Chocolate River did look melted," Cocoa told Raina.

Dash's silver wings flapped nervously. "Last night, I heard howling and moaning in Peppermint Grove," she whispered.

"Something isn't right in Sugar Valley," Melli muttered. "Oh, and there's so much to do! Think of all the fall candy crops that could be ruined."

"Let's not get our wings dipped in syrup yet," Berry told her friends. "We can get to the bottom of this."

A sugar fly buzzed up and dropped a note for Raina. She read the letter quickly and then showed her friends. "The note is from Candy Castle. Princess Lolli is calling a meeting for all of the fairies. We are supposed to go to the Royal Gardens at Candy Castle *now*."

Melli gasped and her hand flew to her mouth.

"If Princess Lolli is calling us to the castle, the situation has to be really sour!" Dash exclaimed.

"Not necessarily," Cocoa said, trying to keep her friends calm. But in her heart, she wasn't so sure. Princess Lolli was the kind and gentle ruler of all of Sugar Valley. She didn't often call a meeting with all the fairies unless something was *very* urgent.

The fairies flew off to Candy Castle hoping that all would soon be right in the Sugar Valley.